I See a Bear, but...

Evelyn—
I hope you have an amazing holiday and enjoy your bear adventure.
KA Morgan

K.A. Morgan

INSPIRE Books

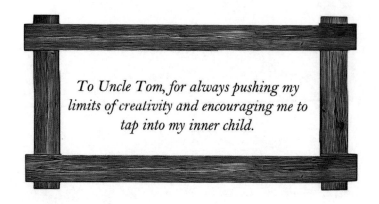

To Uncle Tom, for always pushing my limits of creativity and encouraging me to tap into my inner child.

Inspire Books
A Division of Inspire Creative Services
937 West 1350 North, Clinton, Utah 84015, USA

An Inspire Book published by arrangement with the author

First Inspire Books paperback edition November, 2015

I SEE A BEAR, BUT...

Summary: Illustrations and humorous rhyming text portray a young child's walk through a forest and several animals seen along the way.

ISBN-13: 978-1-939049-20-9
ISBN-10: 1939049202

Printed in the United States of America

I see a bear, but...

he doesn't see me...

because he's too busy...

taking honey from bees.

I see a moose, but...

he doesn't see me...

because he's too busy...

grazing on weeds.

I see a wolf, but...

he doesn't see me...

because he's too busy...

scratching at fleas.

I see a squirrel, but...

he doesn't see me...

because he's too busy...

collecting nuts in a tree.

I see a bunny, but...

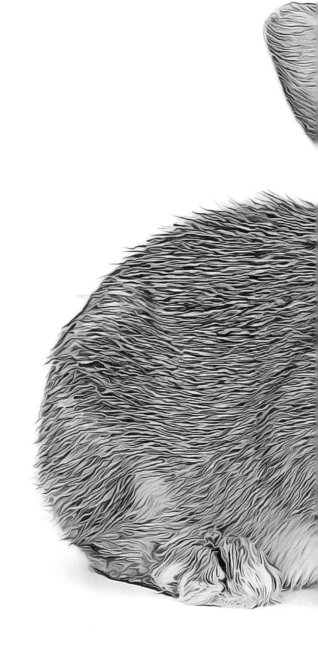

he doesn't see me...

because he's too busy...

hiding in leaves.

I see a deer, but...

he doesn't see me...

because he's too busy...

eating berries.

I see a raccoon, but...

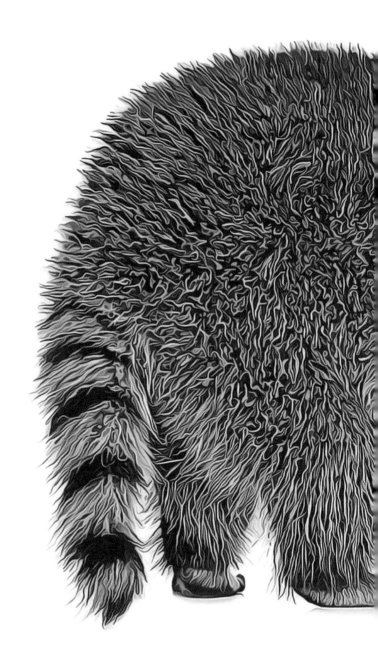

he doesn't see me...

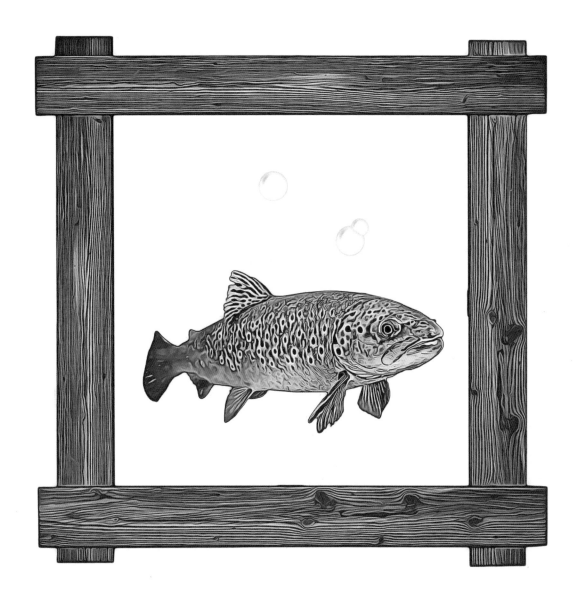

because he's too busy...

fishing upstream.

I see a skunk, but...

he's LOOKING at me...

spitting, and growling,
 and stamping his feet...

I think I'll just go now.

I better retreat.

TOO LATE!

His tail lifts and
sprays me with stink.

PEW-EE!!

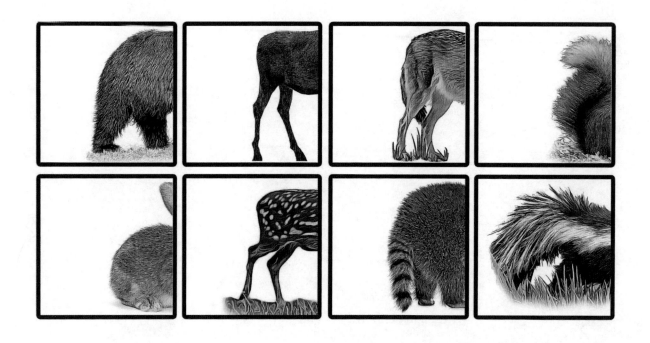

The End!

51252419R00022

Made in the USA
Charleston, SC
13 January 2016